SHARK ISLAND

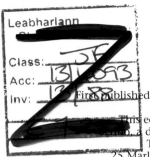

First published in France by Éditions Flammarion MMVI

This edition published by Scribo MMX,
a division of Book House, an imprint of
The Salariya Book Company
25 Marlborough Place, Brighton, BN1 1UB
www.book-house.co.uk
www.salariya.com
www.scribobooks.com

ISBN 978-1-907184-53-6

The right of Alain Surget to be identified as the author of this work and
the right of Annette Marnat to be identified as the illustrator of this work
has been asserted in accordance with sections 77 and 78 of the Copyright,
Designs and Patents Act, 1988.

Printed and bound in China

Translated by Jill Lewin

Editor: Shirley Willis

The text for this book is set in 1Stone Serif
The display types are set in OldClaude

Written by
Alain Surget

Illustrated by
Annette Marnat

Translated by
Jill Lewin

SHARK ISLAND

Chapter I

Destination – Les Cayes

Hispaniola! The name sounded like the title of a Spanish song. For many days now they had been sailing the Caribbean Sea and Benjamin and his sister Louise had not been able to get the name out of their heads. Hispaniola! Hispaniola! It was there, in the town of Les Cayes, that they hoped to find their father, the notorious pirate Captain Roc. The father whom they'd never known and who had had each of the twins' shoulders tattooed with part of a treasure map when they were born. Standing at the prow of the Angry Flea – the ship snatched from the pirate Black Beard – their eyes were glued to the island ahead. Outlined against the sky was a strip of coconut palms stretching out into the sea, with hills in the background.

'We're almost there at last!' sighed Louise.

Benjamin didn't reply at once. Knowing that the father they'd been searching for was within close reach, on this sliver of land that barely rose above the ocean, seemed to him about as unlikely as if he'd been told that he could reach out and touch the moon. Yet this really was Hispaniola, their destination. Its white houses, which could be seen through the trees, were reflected in the sparkling sea.

'Over on the right there is Île à Vache!' he said eventually, pointing about five miles beyond Hispaniola to a mass of rocks that looked more like a collection of shells. 'That's father's hideout.'

'First, we'll make landfall at Les Cayes,' said the ship's captain, the Marquis Roger de Parabas.

'Aren't we in danger of being fired on by cannons?' asked Benjamin. 'After all, we are in Black Beard's ship!'

'There are more pirates in the town than Spanish soldiers,' chuckled Parabas.

'How does that work?'

'Pirates are tolerated in Hispaniola as long as they turn over part of their booty to the governor of the island,' Parabas explained.

'That doesn't make me feel any better,' Benjamin continued, 'because we've got nothing to share with him.'

'We'll put up a fight!' declared Louise, pretending to draw a sabre from her belt. 'I've always dreamt of taking part in a good old tavern brawl!'

'You can do what you like,' said Benjamin, 'but I'm going off to find a quiet corner to finish my book!'

'Huh! Bookworm!' his sister scoffed, pulling a disdainful face.

'Hmm! You think you're so clever, dressed like a man, but you handle a sabre as if you're cutting sausages.'

'Hush, you two!' Parabas cut in. 'I will go to Les Cayes alone to look for Cap'n Roc. You'll be staying here with the crew.'

'Why's that?' demanded Louise, crossing her arms. 'He's our father, after all!'

'Because that's what I've decided,' said the marquis, looking her straight in the eye. 'This town isn't safe. Wherever pirates hang out is no place for children.'

'But we're pirates too, my brother and I!'

'Don't disobey me, or you'll be in for a roasting!'

'You'll be hung from the main mast, son of a sharrrk!' squawked Shut-your-trap! the parrot, perched on the captain's shoulder.

'And you can stay here, too!' Parabas ordered him. 'I certainly don't need a town-crier when I go into Les Cayes.'

'No drrrum? No trrrumpet?' questioned the surprised parrot.

'Exactly! And if you do follow me, I'll tell Lard-Head, the cook, to roast you when I get back.'

'Trrraitorrr! Barrrbarrrian! Cannibal!' screeched Shut-your-trap! as he made for the safety of the rigging.

The Angry Flea entered the bay of Les Cayes. Two small boats lurched about on the waves, and several ships lay at anchor close to the harbour.

A large merchant vessel, moored at the quayside, was loading a cargo of exotic products bound for Spain.

'Which is father's ship?' asked Louise, as Parabas looked at the boats through his telescope.

'I can't see it.'

'Oh!' sighed Louise, clearly disappointed.

'What's his ship called?' she asked.

'The Marie-Louise. She's a two-masted brigantine, rather similar to this ship.'

'That's our mother's first name and mine!' she cried proudly. 'Can I have a look through your telescope?'

Parabas handed it over to her. Louise scanned the anchored ships, hoping to spot her father's vessel behind a sail or half-hidden by another ship.

'Perhaps father is ashore!' she murmured, refusing to admit the possibility that he wasn't there.

'I'll be checking, anyway,' Parabas reassured her.

'Or maybe he's on Île à Vache,' Benjamin added.

'Don't worry, I'll ask around. On-the-Fence!' he yelled.

His first mate, On-the-Fence, arrived at the double.

'Launch the rowing boat and pick out two men to row for me. Then get the ship away from the coast, out of range of those cannons on the citadel. You never know what might happen on land. Come back at nightfall. And have these two watched by Scarface and One-Eyed Jack,' he added in a low voice. 'I don't want them to get up to anything stupid in an attempt to find their father.'

'We've only got one boat, and you're taking it,' responded the first mate. 'If they try to swim to the port, they won't make ten strokes. This sea is full of sharks!'

'You're responsible for their safety. Understand?' growled Parabas.

'I suppose so,' grumbled On-the-Fence, shrugging his shoulders.

Moments later, Benjamin and Louise watched as the rowing boat pulled away, the ship's ropes groaned as they turned in their pulleys and the sails pivoted to catch the west wind. The ship turned on her keel and set her prow towards Île à Vache.

'This is driving me mad!' groaned Louise, thumping the ship's rail with her fists. 'Father might be so close, but we're heading away from him!'

'Parabas will bring him here this evening if he finds him,' her brother reassured her. 'But... if father is on Île à Vache, we're actually getting closer to him.'

'Oh!' Louise grumbled. 'I don't know how you can stay so calm. I'm as jumpy as a flea. I can't keep still. Doing nothing is making me crazy!'

She glanced at the two pirates leaning against the mast behind them. As their gaze met hers, she had the uncomfortable feeling that their smiles looked shark-like. Suddenly, for the first time, it crossed her mind that she and Benjamin might be prisoners.

Chapter II

A boarding party!

The Angry Flea dropped anchor about a mile from the port. Benjamin and Louise had not stopped looking back towards Les Cayes since the ship had turned, as if they were afraid that the town might disappear into the sea.

'If father isn't in Les Cayes or on Île à Vache either, what on earth are we going to go?' asked Louise.

'We'll wait for him, for goodness sake!' her brother snapped.

'Wait? Wait?' exclaimed Louise. 'I've had quite enough of waiting!' Turning around, she spotted On-the-Fence talking with the helmsman. She went across to them.

'Since we've got to hang around till nightfall,

why don't we sail around Île à Vache to see if the Marie-Louise is anchored there?'

'Out of the question!' snapped the first mate. 'The cap'n ordered us to wait here, then to go back for him. He didn't authorise me to go off exploring.'

'But he won't know!' Louise insisted.

'There are reefs in the shallows hereabouts,' the helmsman cut in. 'I doubt whether any ship could land on the island without being broken up. We'd need a small boat to thread its way in carefully.'

'Who said anything about landing?' pleaded Louise, her foot tapping. 'I just said we should sail around the island.'

'If your father has gone to his hideout, he's gone by rowing boat and not with the Marie-Louise,' replied On-the-Fence. 'There are so many little creeks to hide a small boat in that no one sailing along the coastline would see it.'

'But if father is on the island, his ship can't be far away,' Louise continued obstinately, not yet having exhausted her argument. 'Parabas will appreciate it if you can tell him if the Marie-Louise is cruising in the vicinity or not.'

'Parabas will punish us,' the helmsman corrected her. 'He doesn't tolerate people disobeying his orders!'

'Parrrabas will punish us!' repeated Shut-your-trap! He had flown back down and was hopping around between their feet. 'He'll hang you from the yarrrd...'

'Hey, that's enough out of you!' Louise shouted at him. 'Or I'll hang you by your claws in place of the ship's bell!'

The parrot took refuge behind Benjamin, squawking and hiding his head under his wing.

'Ahoy!' the boy suddenly yelled. 'There's a boat approaching and I think it's full of armed men.'

'Soldiers?' demanded the bosun.

'I can't see any helmets or breastplates,' Benjamin shouted back.

The pirates crowded against the ship's rail to take a look.

On-the-Fence peered at the newcomers through

his eyeglass. 'They're buccaneers like us,' he announced. 'I wonder what they want. Bosun, put the men on alert!'

'Shall I open the gun ports and aim the cannons?'

'No, we'd have to weigh anchor to take them with firepower. We don't have time for that. Hoist the sails and make a quarter turn.'

The bosun turned round and shouted at the top of his voice:

'To your swords and pistols! Battle stations!'

'Some action at last!' rejoiced Louise. 'Give me a weapon, too!'

'No way,' said On-the-Fence without hesitation. 'If it gets dangerous, you and your brother are to take refuge in the cap'n's cabin!'

'And defend ourselves by hitting people with books and charts?' Louise protested. 'At least give me a knife or a hammer – or a lump of wood.'

But On-the-Fence didn't reply. He was watching the small boat approaching. Its occupants had folded back the lateen sail to slow the boat down.

Now they were rowing it towards the Angry Flea. On-the-Fence was leaning over the railing, backed up by a show of pistols.

'What do you want?' he shouted in a menacing voice.

'You've got a lovely ship there,' said the pirate who stood at the front of the boat. 'I'm sure you could do with extra men for your crew. Put down your arms and send over a rope ladder.'

'We've got a full crew! Go back to Les Cayes!' On-the-Fence told them.

The fellow's eyebrows creased into a frown.

'We're bored on dry land. And we've run out of money. A little expedition against a town in Jamaica or Panama would refill our coffers!'

On-the-Fence shook his head. 'Get out of here!' he shouted, shaking his fist, his pistol clutched in it.

'Think about it,' said the pirate, persisting. 'We're good fighters. You wouldn't regret...'

One of the pirate's companions muttered:

'You're wasting your time – he'll never let us on board. On the other hand, we need this ship.'

With pistols at the ready and blades shimmering, their faces were tense with anticipation as two bands of pirates stared each other out for a few moments. Then a gunshot rang out. The fight had started! Grappling hooks flew through the air and fixed onto the ship's rail. Rifles cracked, bodies swayed and shouts went up as the intruders boarded the ship, breaking through its defences

and reaching the deck. Pistol shot was flying everywhere. The crew resorted to using their empty weapons as clubs.

Perched on a barrel, Louise was making gestures to encourage the crew and egging them on loudly, whilst her brother was trying to make her come down. On-the-Fence lunged forward suddenly, grabbed her by the waist and pulled her from her perch.

'Take shelter!' he growled. 'Or do I have to knock you out to make you obey orders?' he shouted over Louise's protests.

Just then he turned to ward off an attack. Benjamin dragged his sister towards Parabas' cabin whilst On-the-Fence was climbing into the rigging to get a better vantage point. As fresh volleys rang out they were punctuated by cries of pain. The air was filled with the smell of gunpowder and smoke and the deck was strewn with bodies.

Benjamin slammed the cabin door behind him.

'There are a lot fewer still standing now, but they're fighting just as hard,' he told his sister.

'Hey, what are you doing?'

Louise had opened the rear porthole just under the poop deck, and was leaning out.

'I can see the pirates' boat,' she said. 'If we climb along this ledge under the porthole, we should be able to get to it.'

'Why? What have you got in mind?' Benjamin asked, suspecting the worst.

'The only way to find out if father is on Île à Vache is to go there ourselves and look for him.'

'And if he isn't?'

'We'll wait. It'll be less boring on the island than here on the ship. Father will turn up eventually. He must have some stores of food in his hideout. We don't need Parabas to help us find him!'

'But what if father's in Les Cayes?'

'Now I think about it, I don't believe he's in town. His ship, the Marie-Louise, would have been in the port. But if he's there after all, he'll know to find us on his island. Let's go before the boat drifts off or the pirates jump back into it to escape.'

'I don't know if this is such a good idea!' Benjamin said hesitantly.

'To the devil with good ideas!' announced Louise. 'I've had enough of slaving away on the Angry Flea. Freedom...'

Crash! The door flew open against the wall. The pirate who had just given it a mighty kick was framed in the doorway.

'Dear, dear!' he chuckled. 'Two little pigeons trying to fly away!'

Rushing towards the children, he knocked Benjamin over as he dived at Louise to prevent her escaping through the porthole. She screamed and tried to defend herself by kicking, punching, scratching and biting. Thwack! Suddenly, the man slumped and let go of her. His mouth gaped and his eyes were rolling. Another dull thwack resounded and he sank to his knees. Standing behind him was Benjamin, brandishing the ship's manual in both hands and about to bring it down hard for a third time on the fellow's skull. There was a loud crash as the pirate collapsed, unconscious.

'Well done!' Louise exclaimed.

'So I've finally managed to show you how useful books are!' said Benjamin proudly.

'Well, they're certainly a good way of getting things into your head!' laughed Louise as she grabbed the man's sabre. 'Now let's get out of here while we can.'

She clambered through the porthole and stood on the wooden ledge below. The sound of movement coming from the cabin spurred Benjamin on to follow his sister. Clinging to the hull, the children slid one foot in front of the other to make their way slowly forward. A body brushed past them as it fell overboard, making Benjamin cry out with shock. He lost his balance and flapped his arms about wildly. As Louise grabbed hold of him she saw a grey fin cut through the water towards the ship.

'Sharks!' she shivered.

'There are loads of them,' Benjamin warned as he spotted the silver shapes darting around the Angry Flea.

The small boat bobbed on the waves about a metre from the ship. High up on deck, the fight was now subsiding. The last of the attackers were being rounded up around the main mast.

'We'll have to jump,' said Louise.

'Are you mad? The boat's rocking like crazy, you...'

Whoosh! Louise had thrown herself forward. She fell backwards into the boat and the impact made it roll violently from side to side. Instinctively, she grabbed the little mast to save herself from being tossed into the sea. Benjamin leapt after her. They each grabbed an oar and pulled hard on it in an effort to move the boat away from the Angry Flea.

'We've done it!' said Louise with a sigh of relief. 'From now on, we don't need to rely on anyone.'

Just then the parrot dived towards them.

'Billy goat's horrrn! Escaping? Parrrabas...'

'Shut your trap!' ordered the children in unison.

'Or I'll roast you alive!' Louise chipped in.

The tone of her voice silenced the bird in mid-squawk. He took refuge on top of the mast, buried his head in his feathers and let out a muffled croak, more out of rage than fear.

Chapter III

Too close
for comfort

On the ship, the sound of fighting had stopped. The dead and wounded from both sides had been thrown below decks. A figure suddenly appeared on the poop deck waving its arms in the children's direction.

'They're beckoning us back,' said Benjamin.

'They can wave and shout till they're blue in the face, but we're not turning back!' Louise replied. 'I've decided to go to the island to find father, and no-one's going to stop me.'

'On-the-Fence will come after us!'

'Well, we'll just have to make sure he doesn't find us!'

Benjamin put down his oar, undid the sail ropes and hoisted it into the wind. The boat sped along, leaping over the waves. Benjamin took the tiller whilst his sister positioned herself where she could keep an eye on the Angry Flea's movements.

'They're letting out the ropes,' she told Benjamin. 'The sails aren't full yet, but the helmsman is manoeuvring the ship so that it will catch the wind.'

'The Angry Flea's a heavy ship,' Benjamin explained. 'She'll move off slowly, but once she sets sail she'll pick up speed.'

Louise didn't look round. Her attention was fixed on two triangular shapes that had just emerged above water.

'It's not Parabas' men giving chase that we need to worry about,' she stated, her throat dry.

Benjamin looked over his shoulder. The two black shapes grew larger in the wake of the boat. Sharks!

'I'll tie the tiller in place and keep the sail steady so we can both start rowing again. We'll move faster like that.'

'We might outrun a ship, but not sharks.'

'I know. I just hope that the splashing of the

oars will keep them at bay and stop them attacking the hull.'

They sat, crouched side by side, and pulled on the oars.

'There are so many of them!' murmured Benjamin. He was filled with panic, seeing the sea bristling with fins. 'Should we head back to the Angry Flea?'

'No way!' spat Louise. 'The island isn't far, and these horrible fish can't jump into the boat.'

For a while, the sharks seemed content to follow the boat, fanning out around it. Suddenly, a loud noise split the air followed by a whistling sound. Then a waterspout shot up just behind the boat.

'Oh no! The Angry Flea's firing on us,' cried Louise. 'It's a warning... or maybe On-the-Fence ordered the gunners to fire a round to disperse the sharks.'

The waves breaking around the island created a barrier of foaming surf.

'We're getting close to the reefs,' Benjamin warned. 'I'll lower the sail and take the tiller again. You go up front and guide me through the rocks! This boat has a flat bottom, so we should be able to get through.'

Louise helped her brother bring down the sail and tied it to the mast.

'Hey!' she exclaimed suddenly. 'All the fins have disappeared.'

'That's because of the reef, or perhaps the cannon ball scared them off,' Benjamin explained. 'The Angry Flea won't risk coming any closer.'

The sea crashed over the reef with a terrible thundering noise. The first of the jagged rocks were now visible under the water.

'Son of a sharrrk! That'll rrrock the boat!' screeched Shut-your-trap!

'There are times when I wish I was a bird,' murmured Louise, crouching at the front of the boat.

Leaning forward, she plunged her oar straight down into the water to gauge its depth. Suddenly it was wrenched from her hands. She screamed in terror and barely had time to jump back as a shark's snout shot up out of the sea, snapped its jaws around the gunwale and tore off a piece of the wood. The oar bobbed to the surface again, torn to shreds.

'They're attacking!' Louise shrieked.

The sharks lunged at the hull and sunk their teeth into it, shaking it to tear off pieces of the planking.

'Push them back!' yelled Benjamin. 'If I leave the tiller, we'll end up on the reef.'

Louise grabbed the other oar and struck out with it as hard as she could to the right and left. The sharks' teeth crunched against the oar and they dived only to renew their attack once more. The sharks nudged the boat in an attempt to topple its occupants into the water. Louise suddenly dropped the oar and pulled the sabre from her belt.

'It's too short,' Benjamin warned her. 'The sharks will have your arm off!'

Just then the boat jolted to a stop with a sudden bang. It had hit the reef. A loud scraping noise made the whole boat frame shudder. 'We've had it!' Benjamin thought.

'Take that!'

Louise put all her strength into the blow. The sword blade plunged into the back of a huge shark and broke off. The creature lurched up and then dived, leaving a trail of blood. The other sharks instantly raced forwards to attack it. And that did it! The water turned red. The sharks, now in a feeding frenzy, fought each other and ignored the boat above them.

'Fantastic!' Benjamin exclaimed. But the boat was taking water.

Benjamin ripped off his jacket and stuffed it into the hole. Louise then grabbed the oar and, positioning herself at the front again, she used it to

guide the boat between the rocks. The backwash from a wave dragged the boat towards a rock. The stern hit the reef and was holed yet again. As the boat turned, a stronger wave lifted it right over the reef.

'We're through!' cheered Louise.

'But we're sinking,' her brother warned. 'The water's rising really fast.'

Weighed down by the water it had taken on, the boat was slowing down and was indeed sinking.

'The sharks are busy with their feast now, we can swim to the island,' said Louise. 'We're almost there.'

The twins jumped into the sea and soon covered the short distance to shore. They lay flat out on the sand for a few minutes, exhausted. When they did look up and glanced over their shoulders, they saw that their boat had sunk and that the Angry Flea had now appeared beyond the reef.

'On-the-Fence must be looking at us through his telescope,' Benjamin murmured.

'Doesn't matter! The ship can't make it through

the reef and the rowing boat is in Les Cayes. On-the-Fence will pick up Parabas later, but no pirate would dare tackle the reef at nightfall. We're okay until tomorrow... Just think, we're on father's island. We're home! We're home!' Louise repeated, rolling around in the sand like a puppy.

Chapter IV

Île à Vache

The children had begun making their way to the highest point of the island so they could get a view of the whole place. Île à Vache was covered with thick, luxurious vegetation with jagged rocky outcrops that made it look like a dinosaur's back.

'I can see why father has chosen this as his hiding place' Benjamin said. 'You could hide things just about anywhere here!'

'Yes, but that means we don't know where to look.'

Louise stopped dead and grabbed her brother by the arm.

'What if he's set traps everywhere?' she asked in a worried voice.

Alerted by this thought, they now began looking around as they walked. The island suddenly seemed very hostile. What was shaking those tall ferns? Did something just slither by in the grass? Why was that palm tree swaying? Was there something climbing it? Was that an arrow pointing out of the bush over there... or just a branch? And what was that strange shape over there? Was that someone crouching behind the rock?

'It's just the shadow of the palm tree,' Benjamin reassured Louise, pointing at the tree. 'And the birds are making the leaves move.'

'What about that humming sound? Can't you hear it? That's not normal!'

'It's just the sound of the sea.'

'It sounds as though it's echoing underneath our feet and making the island vibrate - it's as if the rocks are speaking to us.'

'I expect there are plenty of underground caves and passages. They must get flooded whenever the tide comes in,' said Benjamin, logically.

'I think they're ghost caves,' Louise insisted. 'Guardians of our father's treasure.'

'You just love scaring yourself!' laughed Benjamin.

'Yeah!' she confessed, smiling. 'It gives me goose bumps and it makes me want to scream out all my anxiety. Don't you feel like that too, after the fright we had with those sharks?'

'Well yes, maybe it would do us some good,' Benjamin agreed.

So they let out a howl, long and loud like a wolf, and then let rip with all sorts of wild animal noises. At the sound of it, a flock of birds flew up in panic and several jibbering monkeys ran to the tops of the trees.

'Repel boarrrderrrs! To arrrms! Prrreparrre to firrre!' screeched Shut-your-trap!, joining in with the commotion.

'Father, it's us! Benjamin and Louise!' they bellowed.

But there was silence. The island remained quiet except for the sound of the sea lapping against the rocks and the waves rolling endlessly onto the beach.

'There's no one here,' said Louise, disappointed.

They began climbing again and when they reached a rocky outcrop they stopped to take a good look around them.

'It's sort of banana-shaped,' declared Benjamin 'I wonder why it's called Cow Island?'

'It's a funny kind of name. Let's call it Shark Island instead... Anyway, I'm thirsty, hungry and exhausted!'

Shielding their eyes with their hands, they surveyed each section of the island.

'The Angry Flea's keeping her distance,' Benjamin noted. 'On-the-Fence knows we're trapped here!'

Louise shrugged her shoulders. From now on, this was where they'd be living. A nearby waterfall had caught her brother's attention as it tumbled down between the palm trees like a long bridal veil.

'Lets go that way,' he decided. 'Father's hiding place must be near fresh water.'

'And in a place that's easy to defend,' Louise chipped in. 'A place where he can see out, but not be seen.'

Before renewing their search, they broke open several coconuts with a stone, drank the milk and ate the coconut flesh. They allowed themselves a little while to rest before setting off again. The

island wasn't very big and they soon came across a stream, scaring off a family of little pigs which ran away squealing.

'I can hear the sound of the waterfall,' Benjamin said, 'so we must be nearly there.'

And what a waterfall! Gushing from the side of the hill, it tumbled and splashed over a jumble of rocks and formed a natural pool below.

'The last one in the water's a donkey!' cried Louise, slipping off her shoes.

Clothes flew everywhere and Benjamin dived in first.

'I won!' he shouted, surfacing.

'Huh!' replied Louise. 'That's because you had less clothes to take off.'

Then she, too, jumped into the water with a great splash!

They swam for some time before Benjamin stretched himself out on a rock to dry off. Louise, meanwhile, started ferreting about.

'Benjamin, come and see!' she called suddenly. 'There's a narrow track behind the waterfall.'

'A trrrack? In the rrrock? Billy goat's horrrn! It's the jaws of hell!' warned Shut-your-trap!, taking refuge on a high branch.

Benjamin joined his sister.

'That's odd,' she said, 'there's daylight shining behind the rock face as if there's an opening.'

The gap wasn't very big, but they managed to get through, crawling for part of the way. To their surprise they ended up in a cave. Daylight shone in from above through a sort of chimney that had been carved out and widened over the centuries by violent tropical downpours.

'Goodness!' Louise gasped. 'I bet this is father's hideout!'

Four barrels were stacked against the rockface alongside a woodpile as well as an axe, a sabre and an old musket. Planks of wood were placed across sections of tree trunk to form a makeshift table on which stood an oil lamp, a tinderbox and two or three knives. A large boulder served as a seat, and a mattress of leaves as a corner bed. A cover was spread over the barrels, canvas bags hung from a hook fixed into the rock, and a dozen stones marked out a hearth filled with ashes.

'I had expected something more like a log cabin or a small fort,' said Louise, sounding disappointed.

Benjamin's voice, on the other hand, vibrated with excitement as he said:

'Father must have been here fairly recently. Look, there's no dust on the table.'

Louise lifted a goblet and ran her finger over the round mark it had left on the table.

'Still sticky,' she said. 'Possibly honey or molasses, or...'

'Or rum,' explained her brother, removing a cork from a bottle.

'You're right, father must have been here two or three days ago at the most!'

'There's dried meat in these bags,' said Benjamin. 'So we won't die of hunger... Hey, what are you doing?' he asked, noticing his sister tucking the sabre into her belt. Then she lifted the musket and held it out to him.

'Let's carry on exploring. Maybe father's still on the island. I'm sure he must have several hiding places.'

The children set off across the island, armed like real pirates. But, apart from a herd of cows and a few wild goats, they didn't discover anything, certainly not a cabin or cave which could have sheltered Captain Roc.

'We're not doing this right!' grumbled Louise. 'We're not searching, we're just having a walk.'

'If he does have other hiding places, they're very well hidden. We'll need a lot of time to find him.'

'We'll move every rock if we have to, but we will find him!' Louise suddenly had an idea.

'What if we make a big fire? If father is on the island, that would bring him out of his hiding place or... if he's sailing around the island, he'd see it and come to investigate. It's getting dark, so he could easily see it from a distance.'

'Unfortunately, so would the soldiers in Les Cayes – and so would other pirates, too,' Benjamin pointed out. 'Father would never forgive us for attracting the whole world to his island!'

'That's true. The only thing we can do is go back to the waterfall before it gets dark,' Louise muttered.

They set off again, disappointed not to have found any trace of their father. When they got back to the cave, Louise embedded the point of her sabre in the table and flopped down, disgruntled. Benjamin cut himself a slice of meat and began to chew.

'What about tomorrow?' he asked. 'Parabas will come looking for us. Do we go back on board with him, or wait here for father to show up?'

'That will depend on what Parabas has to tell us. If he knows exactly where father is, we'll go back to the Angry Flea. If not...'

She left her sentence unfinished. For the moment, the only sound to be heard was Benjamin chewing on a piece of dried meat.

'Aren't you hungry? Do you want me to cut you some meat – or do you want some water?'

Louise shook her head.

'I'm wondering what father is like.'

'Parabas has already described him to us – tall, with a beard...'

'No, I mean his character or... whether he has a sparkle in his eye. I don't think he'd treat us like he does his crew. What will it be like when he does see us?'

Lying on her back, Louise put her hands behind her head and started to hum.

'That's the tune Mum used to sing,' said Benjamin, recognising it. 'She said father taught it to her.'

Together, the children sang:

The sailor leaves port
In the finest of ships
In his heart
Are three flowers
On his shoulder, a bird sits

It's there, his most treasured
Not the ends of the Earth
In his heart
Are three flowers
On his head a big hat

Chapter V

A change
of direction

At dawn the next day, a loud booming noise resounded over the sea. Boom! Boom! Boom!

'All hands on deck!' screeched Shut-your-trap! as he flapped his wings at the children. 'Charrrge the cannons! It's all kicking off!'

With such a rude awakening, Benjamin and Louise took a few seconds to react.

'Do you think it's the Angry Flea?' asked Louise, throwing back the covers.

'I don't know... the cannons sound different.'

'I hope it's not the Marie-Louise under attack from enemy ships. We can't lose father just as we're about to find him!'

They rushed from the cave and ran towards the shore.

'Stop!' shouted Benjamin. It would be better if we climbed up on those rocks over there. We'll be able to see just as well, but they'll shelter us from stray shots.'

When they'd scrambled up the jagged rock overhanging the coconut palms they saw an extraordinary sight; a ship was broadside on to the Angry Flea and both were firing ferociously at each other.

'It's a sloop,' said Benjamin, 'a single-masted ship. But it's faster and more manoeuvrable than the Angry Flea. It's been positioned between Parabas' ship and the island to stop her approaching.'

'So why doesn't Parabas just sink it?' exclaimed Louise impatiently.

Boom! Boom! Boom! The other ship fired another round, but the Angry Flea had moved further away. A wall of water shot up in front of her. In response, there was a noise like a roll of thunder as all Parabas' cannons spat out their shot, engulfing their ship in thick smoke. The sea was alive with the onslaught of cannonballs and the prow of the sloop splintered in a shower of debris.

'Gotcha!' trumpeted Louise.

'That's not enough to put the sloop out of action! It's turning, it's lining up its cannons... Oh no, in that position it will smash the Angry Flea's hull.'

'Look - Parabas is turning, too. But that's...

impossible!' sighed Louise. 'He's running away. He's abandoning us, the coward.'

'Scarrredy cat! Pumpkin! Earrrthworrrm!' added Shut-your-trap!

'Look, those figures on the sloop are waving.'

'They're jumping for joy, I expect!'

'That's not all,' said Benjamin, 'look what they're doing now. They're lowering a rowing boat in the water.'

'It's us they're looking for,' Louise suddenly realised. 'They're after the pieces of map tattooed on us. Parabas must have blabbed about us in Les Cayes.'

'Quick, let's scarper!' urged her brother. They hurtled down the slope and hid in the deep vegetation. The sloop fired a last victorious broadside as the small boat picked it's way through the reef.

'They're all looking for father's treasure,' panted Benjamin, running towards the waterfall.

'We mustn't let them find us! They mean us no good!' gasped Louise, ducking under an archway of creepers entwined with flowers. 'Aargh!'

Benjamin hurtled into her, almost knocking her over.

'Blimey! Why have you stopped? What...?'

'The question stuck in his throat. An enormous head with huge horns had suddenly appeared through a thicket. The animal, every bit as surprised, stared back at them, but with a look of menace in its eyes. It exhaled noisily, lowered its head and scratched the ground with its hoof.

'Watch out! Brrrigand! Horrrned.... thing!' bawled Shut-your-trap!, flapping around above it.

'Noooo!' cried the children.

Too late. The startled beast charged, horns

lowered. Benjamin and Louise spun on their heels and made a desperate bid to escape. They bounded over ferns, plunged between banana trees, grabbing the trunks to help them make abrupt changes of direction. The thick vegetation slowed them down, but it slowed the cow, too.

'Over here!' called Benjamin, as Louise wrong-footed herself as she wavered between two directions.

She dodged attack by scrambling up onto a big rock, leapt to get back to where Benjamin stood and disappeared underground in a cascade of earth, flowers and small stones. The cow circled the dark hole before trotting off, satisfied. Benjamin rushed towards the hole and threw himself flat on his stomach.

'Louise! Louise!'

She answered but her voice was distorted and echoing.

'It's okay, I'm fine. I'm in a sort of passage, like a corridor. I'll see where it leads.'

'To hell! To hell!' squealed the parrot.

'No, stay where you are! I'll fetch the pirates. So what if they take us prisoner? Can you hear me? Louise – can you hear me?'

No reply. Benjamin didn't know what to do. Go and get help, or wait for Louise to come back. 'What can she see?' he thought. 'It must be as dark as a coal cellar down there!' Just then he saw a light flickering at the bottom of the hole.

'Is that you?' he asked.

'Who do you think it is? I found a torch.'

'A torch? Underground?'

'Come on down. Slide on your back. I'll catch you at the bottom.'

'Are you mad? How are we going to get out?'

'Don't worry,' she bellowed. 'I think I've found father's secret hideout. And since I didn't exactly come in through the front door, there must be another way out.'

'Wow! shouted Benjamin. 'The pirates can search for ever more, they'll never get their hands on us.'

He tore a few leaves off some large plants and stuck them into the ground to cover up the hole. Shut-your-trap! watched him do it, then poked his head under the leaves and peered into the hole, quizzically.

Benjamin's fingers closed around his neck.

'Hey, you. Just follow me – and shut your trap!'

'Help! Strrranglerrr! Barrrbarrrian!' Shut-your-trap's cries were quickly lost in the bowels of the earth.

Chapter VI

The bowels
of the earth

The torch lit up a tunnel, a narrow passageway cut into the rock long ago by an old river. There were clear signs of human occupation. Iron sconces had been fixed to the cavern walls, into which torches were placed.

'Torches coated with tinder,' beamed Louise. 'You just have to strike them against the wall and they light.'

Benjamin took one of the torches down, struck it against the rough rock and it instantly burst into flames.

'Rrrou!' shrieked the parrot, trying to escape.

But Benjamin held him firmly under one arm to prevent him from flying away.

'What have you found?' he asked his sister.

Louise didn't reply but carried on along the passageway in front of him.

'Do you think father installed all these torches? Who cut these steps into the stone?'

'Maybe it was the original inhabitants of the island,' Louise suggested. 'Caribbean Indians, I think. In any case, it's definitely a pirate's lair,' she added, emerging into a large room.

'Crikey!' Benjamin exclaimed.

A vast cavern opened out before their eyes, with more passages leading off that were partly filled with seawater. Little waves lapped around the edge of a pool and there was a glimmer of blueish light showing at the bottom, indicating that daylight was penetrating through a crack in the rocks.

The children grabbed more torches from the walls and shone them round. A whole host of objects appeared. Carved wardrobes, gilded wooden thrones and a mound of chests piled up on top of one another.

'It's father's treasure!' declared Louise. 'Our treasure!'

The sight took Benjamin's breath away. It must have taken years of pirating to amass such riches! Louise ran towards one of the chests. She expected it to be locked, but the lid lifted easily.

'Shirts!' she announced in amazement.

She opened a second one. 'Lace!'

One by one, they opened the lids.

'Linen. Sheets. And a whole load of furniture! We could set up a second-hand clothes and furniture store with this lot.'

'At least I'll have something to wear now,' said Benjamin, choosing a shirt to replace the one he'd left by the side of the pool. 'Father must have stripped half the Americas to have collected so many clothes!' he chuckled. 'The treasure hunters will be very surprised.'

'Parabas was right! He guessed that this place was a decoy. Father's so clever. His booty must be safely hidden somewhere else.'

'Now you can see why they're all so interested in our tattoos,' said Benjamin.

'We're safe as long as they don't find a way in,'

whispered Louise, as if she was suddenly afraid that her words might echo round the vaulted roof and passages.

'I'm afraid they'll remain here on the island till they get their hands on us. So who knows how long we'll have to stay underground.'

'Till father comes back!' Louise declared confidently. 'He'll chase them off!'

'We'd better take a look around. I hope father has laid in some stores of food, too.'

'And guns and weapons. We might need to repel a siege if the enemy does get in!'

'Let's start in that tunnel over there,' Benjamin suggested.

They climbed back up a passageway. Barrels of gunpowder were positioned every fifty paces. Whoever had taken up temporary residence in this place had also planned to blow up the roof in case of danger. Weapons were placed along the tunnel, too – rifles, cutlasses and swords.

'The blades are well oiled and the guns are loaded, too,' Louise confirmed. 'Father was obviously well prepared for a strategic retreat. There are enough weapons here to blow up the whole island. At least we'll have the means to defend ourselves.'

They reached a dead end, retraced their steps and forked off into a passage which opened to the right... only to find themselves back in the big cave again.

'We're going round in circles,' said Louise, stating the obvious. 'We'd better light up torches as we go to stop us going over the same territory'

They ventured into another passageway and found a cache of dried fish wrapped in sailcloth and a barrel full of fresh water.

'We won't die of hunger or thirst,' Benjamin declared, 'but this passage is a dead end, too. We'll have to go back again.'

The children followed yet another passage until they came to a mass of fallen rocks. Retracing their steps, they decided to explore a fourth passageway and got lost in a maze of interconnecting tunnels.

At one point, they thought they could see

daylight at the end of a long corridor, but when they eventually got there it turned out to be the vast cavern yet again.

'I can't go on any more!' sighed Louise, sitting down heavily on a chest.

'I think the tunnels are carved in a star shape around this main cavern and don't lead anywhere else.'

'You mean they're like a spider's web, and we're stuck in it like flies!'

'Let's rest. It's not worth wasting any more effort trying to find another way out. We'll pile chests up underneath the hole we came down, and we'll get out that way.'

But Louise didn't answer. She let out a great sigh, as if emptying herself of all the tension inside her.

'I've never felt so lost,' she admitted. 'I really miss Mum!'

'Me too,' said Benjamin, 'but we've never been so close to our father.'

'Strrrange young birrrds! Weirrrd hatchlings! Orrrph...'

'Hey, you, shut your trap!' ordered the children in unison.

Chapter VII

Beautiful
but deadly

Benjamin and Louise sat patiently on either side of a large chest.

'Do you think the pirates will have reached the island yet?' Benjamin asked.

'I don't know how long we've been here. They could be right above us now.'

'It's the thought that one of them might fall down the hole that scares me.'

'Do you think they'll find the hiding place behind the waterfall?'

'Perhaps they're already there waiting for us!'

Suddenly there was a noise like a stone rolling! The children jumped up. Maybe it was an animal scurrying around in one of the passageways. They listened. They heard nothing but then a faint light emerged from one of the tunnels they hadn't explored.

'They're here!' whispered Louise, instinctively grabbing the parrot and clamping a hand over his beak. Benjamin panicked and wanted to escape along another passage, but Louise thought it best to hide amongst the clothes. They crouched down quickly between the chests, covering themselves with a heap of overcoats, dresses, shirts, bodices, frilly petticoats, bonnets, waistcoats, scarves and shawls.

'If you say a single word, I'll strangle you, you pesky bird!' Louise hissed at Shut-your-trap!

'Rrr..!'

Footsteps were approaching. The children held their breath as two men burst into the cavern.

'Those kids have messed up everything now!' declared a deep voice. Benjamin was staring straight at the point of a sabre close by his head. He was terrified by the thought that the pirates might start thrusting their blades into the pile of clothes in search of them, when the man's voice went on:

'Here's a hat with feathers that would suit me very well.'

'They must be hiding in one of the tunnels,' his companion concluded. 'Let's root 'em out!'

'But where shall we start?'

Louise opened her eyes slightly to peer into the cavern. Both men now stood just a few metres away by the pool. One of them was a tall black man, naked to the waist and wearing the feathered hat he had picked out. He held a sabre in his hand. The other, a Caribbean Indian, was dressed in buckskin and armed with a spear. He was studying the footprints in the dust.

'We'll go that way!' he decided.

The two men moved off.

'It's a good time to escape,' whispered Louise. 'Let's go out the way they came in.'

They stood up, shaking off the pile of clothes that had covered them and...

'I knew you'd be here!' said a voice from behind them. 'I didn't even need to open a wardrobe or move any furniture to find you.'

That voice! They turned to see… Red Mary!

'I promised you we'd meet again!' she said triumphantly. Putting her fingers to her mouth she whistled and the two men reappeared, broad grins on their faces.

'So they took the bait,' chuckled the black man. 'They really believed we'd search all these tunnels!'

'How did you find us?' demanded Louise.

'I reckoned you'd head for Les Cayes to grasp at any chance of finding your father,' explained Mary. 'So my ship intercepted the Angry Flea as it approached Île à Vache. Then I spotted you watching from a rock.'

So you knew about the cavern?' asked Benjamin in amazement.

'I found it long ago by chance, when I was chasing a black pig. I also know there is no treasure here. Malibu, put out these torches in the cave!' she ordered the black man. 'There's a big opening in the rock face at sea level,' she explained to the twins. 'That's why there's light at the end of the pool. But likewise, the torchlight can be seen from outside, too – that's how I knew you were in here. So how did you find this place?'

'We fell down a hole,' Benjamin admitted. 'If you harm us, you'll answer to Parabas!' he added, noticing one of the men drawing his dagger.

'Ha!' scoffed Mary. 'Parabas is a long way from here now so he won't be helping anybody! Anyway, what an earth were you doing in his scheming company?'

'He rescued us from Black Beard and was taking us to our father,' Louise announced.

'And you really believe that's what he was doing?'

'He was father's first mate before he got his own ship,' Louise went on.

'Before betraying him, more like!' Mary corrected her. 'Parabas gave Cap'n Roc up to the English in return for his own life. He's the worst kind of pirate. He's only got one thing on his mind and that's getting his hands on your father's treasure!'

'Is our father imprisoned by the English?' asked Benjamin, dejectedly.

'No. He managed to escape before they shut him away in the fort. If he ever gets his hands on Parabas...'

'He'll end up in little pieces, Parrrabas,' the parrot chipped in for good measure.

'I always had my doubts about him!' Louise thought to herself.

'What about you? What do you want?' Benjamin asked.

'I'm sure you can work that out, can't you?' Mary replied. She called one of the men over. 'Tepos! Show me what I've waited so long to see!'

The man grabbed Benjamin, spun him round and cut off a piece of his shirt. Then he did the same to Louise. Malibu's torch lit up the tattooed maps on the children's shoulders.

'Each of you has a quarter of the map,' said Mary. 'With the half I already have, I will know at last where Cap'n Roc has hidden his treasure!'

'By all the gods!' exclaimed Tepos. 'It's the same as yours!'

'What do you mean it's the same?'

'They've got exactly the same part of the map between them that you've already got on your shoulder.'

'Are you sure?' gulped Mary, her voice becoming shrill.

'I've seen it so often that I know it by heart,' Tepos confirmed.

'What does that mean?' asked Louise. 'Do we have a complete map?'

'No! It means that Cap'n Roc has made fools of us!' Mary raged.

Her eyes narrowed as she met the children's gaze.

'That means you two are worthless to me, now! Tepos, Malibu, get rid of these useless brats!'

Chapter VIII

Blood is thicker
than water

Handing his torch to Red Mary, Malibu took hold of Benjamin and raised his sabre.

'Wait!' shouted Tepos, grabbing his arm. He leaned over to whisper something into Mary's ear in Caribbean dialect, her mother tongue. At first she looked angry and refused, then reluctantly she gave in.

'Okay,' she snarled. 'They can come with us. But I can't protect them from any accidents or enemy bullets.'

They followed one another in single file through a series of passageways until they emerged into the fresh air from behind a big rock hidden by bushes. The two men heaved the rock back in front of the entrance. Then they headed down through the undergrowth to the beach. There was a sudden movement in the tall grasses and ferns and pirates leapt out, pointing rifles at the little group. Tepos and Malibu dropped their weapons. Parabas walked towards Red Mary and took the dagger from her waistband.

'You didn't think I'd left the party, did you?' he smirked. 'We only sailed the Angry Flea away to fool you. In fact, we just went round the island and approached from the other side – and here we are! Just in time, it appears... Has she told you?' Parabas asked the children.

'They know nothing,' muttered Mary.

'Well go on, tell them!'

He drew his sabre, cut the laces that fastened her bodice and bared her left shoulder.

'Let me introduce you to your big sister, or to be more precise... your half-sister. Mary is the daughter of Cap'n Roc and a Caribbean woman!'

Benjamin and Louise stood dumbfounded, their eyes fixed on the map tattooed on Mary's shoulder.

'Cap'n Roc has only ever given away half the

map,' Parabas continued. 'You two got a quarter each, because twins always stick together. So between you, you have half the map. What Mary didn't know was that your father gave you two the same half of the map that he gave to her. The other half is actually on his own back!'

Benjamin turned towards Red Mary.

'Why didn't you tell us you were our sister when we were in Port Royal?' he asked her, aghast.

'I wanted to tell you the truth several times but I wasn't sure how you'd react. You might just have left me in that cell rather than share your father – or his treasure – with me.'

'But how do you know all this?' Louise asked Parabas.

'I lived around Cap'n Roc for a long time, so I discovered all his secrets bit by bit. I found out about Mary's map when she was just a child, without him knowing. You were too little to remember,' he added, glancing at Mary. 'After your mother died, your father left you in the care of your Uncle Tepos and went back to France.'

'So that's why Tepos knew the map better than Mary herself!' Benjamin exclaimed. 'He's had it in front of his eyes for years.'

'Cap'n Roc married again in France and had two more children – you two!' Parabas continued. 'But the call of the sea was too strong. He found a ship and a new crew, and hired me as his first mate.'

Louise realised that her father had named his ship Marie-Louise not just as a reminder of herself and her mother, but his first daughter too.

Suddenly, there was a commotion! A piercing cry from Tepos and Malibu threw everyone off guard. They both surged forward and, knocking the pirates out of the way, they plunged into the thick vegetation. Red Mary took advantage of the momentary confusion to knock Parabas aside and jump over a rock. One of the pirates leapt after

her, but he soon lost her in the maze of creepers and giant foliage.

'She knows the island like the back of her hand,' groaned the marquis. 'No point searching, we won't find her now.'

'I can't believe it!' sighed Louise. 'Mary is our sister, but she was about to kill us back there in the cavern.'

'She's the jealous type,' Parabas commented, removing his topcoat. 'She wants the treasure for herself. She's never forgiven her father for abandoning her.'

'I wonder what Tepos said to her that made her spare us?'

'Caribbean Indians believe that the gods will curse anyone who spills family blood. Tepos probably reminded her of that.'

Parabas signalled to his men to head back towards the sea. As they walked, Louise let Parabas know what was on her mind.

'Mary told us you betrayed our father!'

'Did you believe her?'

'Yes!'

'Well, I had no choice,' Parabas sighed. 'Cap'n Roc sent me and some of the crew ashore. When we came across an English patrol, I saved my own skin by giving them Cap'n Roc. I've always regretted it!'

'Why? Was that because you'd lost half of the treasure map? You must have been overjoyed to hear that he'd escaped.'

'You knew all along that our tattoos of the treasure map were exactly the same as Mary's,' Benjamin went on. 'That's why you never bothered to look at ours. We trusted you, but you only saved us from Black Beard to use us as bait to catch our father!'

'You're no different from Black Beard,' spat Louise. 'You're only interested in the treasure.'

'Once a pirate, always a pirate!' Parabas admitted. 'But right now, could you both shut up?'

'Not before we know what you intend to do. Did you find any news of our father when you were in Les Cayes?'

'Your father, too, is only interested in booty. I heard that the Spanish have found a Mayan city with temples full of gold, and that they're about to load it onto a galleon bound for Seville. They'll embark at Campeche on the coast of New Spain. Cap'n Roc has already set sail in that direction. We're going to follow in his footsteps. I won't let him give me the slip again!' Parabas finished with a cruel smile.

'You really are a villain,' muttered Louise. 'So we're your prisoners?'

As quick as lightning, Parabas brought his sword blade to her throat.

'All that's as may be, but right now, that's quite enough out of you!'

'Underrrstood brrrats? Orrr to the sharrrks with you... Billy goat's horrrn!'

'Take heed of the parrot's words,' the marquis told the children. 'For once, he's giving good advice!'

They reached the shore, where a boat was waiting. The Angry Flea rolled to and fro on the

waves, beyond the reef. Shut-your-trap! settled
himself on Parabas' shoulder, half hidden by his
big hat. Louise reached out and, very sharply, she
yanked a feather from his tail.

'Rrrououou!' screeched the parrot as he shot
into the air.

'Serves you right!' chuckled the twins in unison.

CONTENTS